JUMP THE MOON

To my daughter, Denise, and her pony, Me Too.
—K.S.

To my sister, Renée, who loves horses too.
—M.v.H.

JUMP THE MOON

BY KATHY SIMMERS

ILLUSTRATIONS BY MARJORIE VAN HEERDEN

BOUND TO HAPPEN PUBLISHING, INC.

THERE ONCE WAS A GIRL WITH LONG BLOND HAIR who had always dreamed of having a pony that she could love forever. But she'd never had a pony of her own. She worked long days at a barn, just so she could ride ponies. She thought ponies were perfect, even when they weren't.

One day a scruffy gray pony was brought to the barn for training.

"This is Me Too," said the trainer. "Be careful around her. She'll kick anyone who comes up behind her."

Everyone at the barn was afraid of the pony—everyone except the girl with the long blond hair.

Being the shortest of all her friends, the girl understood that sometimes when you're the littlest, you feel like you have to act tough.

"I think Me Too could be your summer project," the trainer said to the girl with the long blond hair. "I want you to ride her every day."

The girl was so excited that she went to talk to the pony right away.

"I don't think you're really mean, pony," said the girl. "I think you just need someone to be nice to you."

"Me too," thought the pony.

"I'm going to pretend you are *mine*," the girl whispered.

The next day when the girl went to take the pony out of the stall, Me Too pinned back her ears, showed her teeth, and tossed her head.

The girl just patted her and whispered, "I love you, pony."

The girl with the long blond hair took special care of Me Too. She even braided her mane and combed her tail. The pony tried to look mean, but the girl just patted her and said, "I love you, pony."

They went for rides every day.

At first the pony would pin her ears and swish her tail. The girl just patted her and said, "I love you, pony."

Me Too had never trusted people, but there was something different about the girl with the long blond hair. The pony started looking forward to seeing the girl.

After one long ride, the girl said, "I'm hungry. I'd like some cookies."

"Me too," thought the pony.

"I have some special pony cookies just for you!" said the girl.

Nobody had ever shared cookies with the pony before.

The pony started to love the girl with the long blond hair.

The girl and the pony loved going for rides. They especially loved it when they jumped.

"You're a little jumping pony," said the girl. "I feel like we could jump the moon!"

"Me too!" thought the pony.

They went to horse shows, and Me Too didn't look scruffy anymore. Everyone was surprised when they won every class—everyone except the girl with the long blond hair.

"I knew we could do it! I'm so proud of us!" said the girl.

"Me too," thought the pony.

When they were done for the day, they would sit in the hay and eat cookies.

"I love you, pony. I wish we could be together forever."

"Me too," thought the pony.

When summer was over, Me Too had to go back to her old home.

"I'm going to miss you," said the girl with the long blond hair.

"Me too," thought the pony.

"Don't worry, Me Too. I'll see you next summer."

But that didn't happen.

The pony was sold again and again. She moved from home to home, but wherever she lived, nobody made her feel special. Nobody gave her cookies, and nobody ever loved her like the girl with the long blond hair. The pony was lonely and sad. She missed the girl more and more each day.

Then she started to dream about the girl with the long blond hair.

Every night.

The girl with the long blond hair grew up and went to college.

She got married and moved far away.

She didn't ride anymore, but she never forgot Me Too.

Then, suddenly, she started to dream about Me Too.

Every night.

They rode through the woods and jumped logs.

They ate cookies in the hay.

They rode through the stars.

They jumped the moon.

When the girl woke up, she knew.
She *had* to find her pony.

She took the long trip back to the barn where she had ridden Me Too.

"Do you know where I could find Me Too?" she asked.

"You can check at High Hopes Farm," said the trainer.

The girl went to High Hopes Farm, but Me Too wasn't there.

"I sold her to a trainer named Pat," said the owner.

So the girl searched and searched and searched some more until
she found Pat's farm.

But the pony wasn't there.

"I sold her a few years ago to a family with two little girls," said Pat.
"They moved. I have no idea where they are now. I'm sorry."

There was nowhere else to look. The girl went home in tears.

That night she had another dream about Me Too, and she knew that
somehow she would see her pony again.

Pat remembered Me Too. She could tell that someone had once loved that pony. It must have been the girl with the long blond hair.

Pat decided to look for the pony.

One day, as Me Too stood in the rain, Pat came into the field.

"Me Too, I'm so happy I finally found you," she said.

"Me too," thought the pony, and she nickered to Pat.

Pat bought the pony and led her onto a trailer. They went for a *very long* ride.

Finally the trailer stopped. As Me Too backed out of the trailer, Pat said, "I think this looks like a very nice home for a pony."

"Me too," thought the pony.

"I have a surprise for you," said Pat.

Then the pony heard a voice that she would never forget.

"Me Too, it's really you! I could have picked you out of a hundred gray ponies."

The pony's heart leapt! It was the girl with the long blond hair! It was HER GIRL!

The girl gave the pony a big hug. "You were always in my heart," she whispered. "I thought about you every day!"

"Me too," thought the pony.

"I'm ready to go for a ride!"

"Me too!" thought the pony.

They rode across the field, around the pond, and through the woods. They jumped logs until they were so tired that they couldn't jump any more. At the end of the day, the girl rested her face against the pony's and said, "Finally, we are together! Now I know that dreams really do come true."

The pony nuzzled the girl's long blond hair, and of course she thought, "Me too."

This book is based on a true story. When the girl with the long blond hair—whose name is Denise—was fifteen years old, she lived on Long Island and rode with Merilee Ventura at Byway Farms. She spent the summer riding Me Too. The pony was later sold, and life went on.

Seven years later, for no apparent reason, Denise started having dreams about Me Too. She searched for the pony and couldn't find her, but she did find Pat. Pat didn't know where Me Too was either, but she was so moved by Denise's quest that she decided to help. She eventually found the pony in New Jersey and had her brought to Denise's home in North Carolina. There, Denise and Me Too spent their days jumping fences and eating cookies in the hay. And every

KATHY SIMMERS always wanted to live on a farm with horses. When she was twelve years old, she started taking riding lessons. At nineteen she bought her first horse.

Later, as a single, working mother of two, she had to rehome her horse. The farm remained way out of reach. But she never gave up on her dream.

Today Kathy and her husband, Gil, live on a farm in North Carolina with her horses, llamas, a small herd of goats, cats, a dog, and some chickens. It is the life she always dreamed of. You can find her online at www.readjumpthemoon.com

MARJORIE VAN HEERDEN was three months old the first time she "rode" a horse. Her best friend as a child was her horse, Billy Boy.

She grew up on a farm on the southernmost tip of Africa, where she drew what she saw around her: animals and people and dragons and monsters and fairies. Today they appear in her more than 130 children's books. Her award-winning work has been translated into thirty-five languages and has been published in Africa, England, Europe, the United States, China, and Malaysia. You can find her online at www.grafikon.co.za

Delight yourself in the Lord, and He will give you the desires of your heart. —Psalm 37:4